THE OTHER WOMAN

THE OTHER WOMAN

SANDIE JONES

MINOTAUR BOOKS
NEW YORK

THE OTHER WOMAN. Copyright © 2018 by Sandra Sargent. All rights reserved. Printed in the United States of America. For information, address St. Martin's Press, 175 Fifth Avenue, New York, N.Y. 10010.

www.minotaurbooks.com

Designed by Anna Gorovoy

Library of Congress Cataloging-in-Publication Data

Names: Jones, Sandie, author.
Title: The other woman / Sandie Jones.
Description: First edition. | New York : Minotaur Books, [2018]
Identifiers: LCCN 2018011480| ISBN 9781250191984 (hardcover) |
    ISBN 9781250302960 (Canadian) | ISBN 9781250192011 (ebook)
Subjects: LCSH: Women consultants—Fiction. | Man-woman relationships—Fiction. |
    Mothers and sons—Fiction. | Possessiveness—Fiction. | Triangles
    (Interpersonal relations)—Fiction. | GSAFD: Mystery fiction. | Suspense fiction.
Classification: LCC PR6110.O6387 O84 2018 | DDC 823/. 92—dc23
LC record available at https://lccn.loc.gov/2018011480

Our books may be purchased in bulk for promotional, educational, or business use. Please contact your local bookseller or the Macmillan Corporate and Premium Sales Department at 1-800-221-7945, extension 5442, or by email at MacmillanSpecialMarkets@macmillan.com.

10 9 8 7 6 5 4

For Ivy Rolph
My nan—who always encouraged me to be who I wanted to be

THE
OTHER
WOMAN

PROLOGUE

She looks beautiful in her wedding dress. It fits her perfectly and is exactly what I'd imagined she'd go for: elegant, understated, and unique—just like her. My heart breaks that her day will never come, but she doesn't need to know that yet.

I think about the guests who won't attend, the picture frames with no photographs, the first dance that will be silent, the cake that won't get eaten, and I feel my resolve weakening. I pull myself up. This is not a time for doubt.

There is still so much work to do, so much more pain to inflict, but I will not be deterred. I failed once before, but this time, I'll get it right.

There's too much at stake to get it wrong.

ONE

There weren't many things that I didn't like about Adam when I first saw him across the crowded bar at the Grosvenor Hotel in London, aside from his lack of empathy. I'd just come out of an incredibly dull "Future of Recruitment" conference and needed a drink far more than he or the barman realized.

I'd been standing at the bar for what felt like an eternity, theatrically waving a battered ten-pound note in the air, when, just along from me, a dark-haired man muscled his way to the front, holding a credit card. "Yep. Over here, mate," he said in a booming voice.

"Er, excuse me," I said, a little louder than I intended. "I think you'll find I was here first."

He shrugged and smiled. "Sorry, but I've been waiting ages."

I stood and watched openmouthed as he and the barman shared a knowing tip of the head, and without him even saying a word, a bottle of Peroni was put in front of him.

Unbelievable, I mouthed, as he looked over at me. He smiled that smile again, and turned to the throng of men beside him to take their orders.

"You've got to be kidding me," I groaned, before letting my head drop into my arms while I waited. I was sure that it would be an inordinate amount of time until my turn.

"What can I get you?" asked the man behind the bar. "The guy over there reckons you're a rosé kind of girl, but I'm going to bet you're after a gin and tonic."

I smiled despite myself. "As much as I'd like to prove him wrong, I'm afraid to say a glass of rosé would be perfect, please."

I went to hand him the tenner as he placed the glass in front of me, but he shook his head. "No need," he said. "Please accept it with the compliments of the gentleman who jumped the queue."

I didn't know who I loved more: the bartender who, in my opinion, ought to be elevated to chief sommelier, or the really rather nice fellow smiling down the bar at me. Oh, the power of a chilled pink blush.

My face flushed the same color, as I held the glass up to him and headed over to where my seminar colleagues were gathered in a corner, each nursing their own alcoholic preference. We'd been strangers up until seven hours ago, so it seemed that the general consensus was to get your own drink and not worry about everybody else.

Mr. Peroni obviously doesn't have the same arrangement with his own acquaintances, I thought, smiling to myself as I looked up and saw that he had continued to order his round.

I took a sip of wine and could hear my taste buds thanking me as the cold liquid teased them before hitting the back of my throat. What is it with that first taste that can never be replicated? I sometimes find myself postponing that initial swig for fear of losing that sensation.

I'm making myself sound like a raging alcoholic, but I only ever drink on weekends, and on mind-numbingly tedious Wednesdays after being holed up with two hundred HR personnel for the day. We'd been helpfully informed during a lecture entitled "Nobody Likes Us. We Don't Care" that a recent survey had revealed that recruitment consultants were fast becoming the most disliked professionals, second only to real estate agents. I wish I could defy the haters and prove that we weren't all morally lacking, unethical deal makers. But as I looked around at the brash, loud, would-be City boys with their slicked-back hair and insincere expressions, I had to hold my hands up in defeat.

Despite having introduced myself in the "forum" earlier in the day, I felt I had to do it again as I approached the baying mob.

"Hi, I'm Emily," I said awkwardly to the guy in the outermost circle. He wasn't someone I was particularly interested in talking to, but talk I had to, if I wanted to finish my glass of wine without looking like a complete Norman no-mates. "I'm a consultant at Faulkner's," I went on.

I offered my hand and he took it, shaking it brusquely in a slightly territorial fashion. *This is my manor and you're on my turf*, was the message he conveyed, even though we'd spent the entire day learning how to do the exact opposite.

"Be open. Be approachable," Speaker No. 2 had stated earlier. "Employers and employees want to deal with a friendly face. They need to feel that they can trust you. That you are working for them, not the other way around. Deal with your clients on *their* terms, not on yours, even if it does put a dent in your pride. So, read each situation individually and react accordingly."

I'd always prided myself on doing exactly that, hence why I'd been the top consultant at Faulkner's seven months in a row. In person, I was the antithesis of what people expected since I was honest, considerate, and blasé about target-chasing. As long as I had enough to pay my rent, eat, and heat, I was happy. On paper, however, I was smashing it. Clients were requesting to deal exclusively with me, and I'd secured more new business than anyone else across the five-office network. Commissions were flooding in. Perhaps *I* should have been the one standing on that podium, telling them how it's done.

The man, from an obscure agency in Leigh-on-Sea, made a half-hearted attempt at pulling me into the throng. No one introduced themselves, preferring instead to eye me up and down as if seeing a woman for the first time. One of them even shook his head from side to side and let out a slow whistle. I looked at him with disdain, before realizing it was Ivor, the bald, overweight director of a one-office concern in Balham, whom I'd had the misfortune of partnering with in the role-play exercise just before lunch. His breath had smelled of last night's curry, which I'd imagined he'd scoffed impatiently from a silver-foil container on his lap.

"Sell me this pen," he'd barked, during our how-to-sell-snow-to-an-Eskimo task. A cloud of stale turmeric permeated the air, and I wrinkled my nose in distaste. I'd taken a very normal-looking Bic Biro from him and had begun to relay its redeeming qualities: the superior plastic case, the smooth nib, the flow of the ink. I'd wondered, not for the first time, what the point was in all this. My boss, Nathan, insisted that these conferences were good for us: that they kept us on our toes.

If he was hoping that I'd be motivated and captivated by new and exciting ways to do business, he'd booked the wrong day. And I'd certainly been paired with the wrong man.

I'd continued to enthuse about the pen's attributes, but as I'd looked up, Ivor's eyes hadn't even been attempting to look at the tool in my hand, preferring instead to fixate on the hint of cleavage beyond.

"Ahem," I'd coughed, in an attempt to bring his attention back to the task at hand, but he'd merely smiled, as if relishing in his own fantasy. I'd instinctively pulled my blouse together, regretting the decision to wear anything other than a polo neck.

His beady little eyes were still on me now. "It's Emma, isn't it?" he said, stepping forward. I looked down at the name badge secured to my left bosom, just to check for myself.

"Em-i-ly," I said, as if speaking to a toddler. "It's Em-i ly."

"Emma, Emily, it's all the same."

"It's not really, no."

"We were paired up this morning," he said proudly to the other men in the group. "We had a good time, didn't we, Em?"

I'm sure I felt my skin crawl.

"It's Em-i-ly, not Em," I said, exasperated. "And I didn't think we worked particularly well together at all."

"Oh, come on," he said, looking around, his face betraying the confidence in his voice. "We were a good team. You must have felt it." I stared emptily back at him. There were no words of recourse, and even if there were I wouldn't have wasted my breath. I shook my head as the rest of the group looked awkwardly to the floor. No doubt as soon as I turned on my heels they'd be patting him on the back for a job well done.

I took myself and my half-drunk wine to the space at the end of the crowded bar. I'd only been there two minutes before I realized that the reason no one else was standing there was because, every few seconds, I was getting hit in the back by a bony elbow or shouldered out of the way by the waitstaff, as they busily collected drinks and returned glasses. "This is *our* area," barked a young girl, her face all pinched and pointed. "Keep it clear."

"Please," I said under my breath, but she was far too important to stand still long enough to hear it. Still, I edged up a little to remove myself from "her area" and rummaged around in my bag for my phone. I only had three more sips, or one big gulp, of wine left. Four minutes max and I'd be on my way.

I surreptitiously ran through my emails, in the hope that (a) I wouldn't be bothered by anybody and (b) it'd look like I was waiting for someone. I wondered what we'd done before mobiles and their far-reaching information trails. Would I be standing here perusing the *Financial Times* or, better yet, feel inclined to strike up a conversation with someone who might prove to be interesting? Either way, I'd most definitely be better informed as a result, so why, then, did I log on to Twitter to see what Kim Kardashian was up to?

I groaned inwardly as I heard someone shout, "Emily, fancy another drink?" *Really?* Did he not get the hint? I looked over at Ivor, but he was engrossed in conversation. I had a furtive glance around, embarrassed to know that the person who had said it would be watching my confusion. My eyes fleetingly settled on Mr. Peroni, who was grinning broadly, revealing straight white teeth. I smiled to myself as I remembered Mum's erstwhile advice. "It's all in the teeth, Emily," she'd said after she met my last boyfriend, Tom. "You can always trust a man with nice teeth." Yeah—and look how that turned out.

I put more importance on whether someone's smile reaches their eyes, and this guy's, I noticed, definitely did. I mentally undressed him, without even realizing I was doing it, and registered that his dark suit, white shirt, and slightly loosened tie were hanging from a well-built body. I imagined his wide shoulders sitting above a strong back that descended into a narrower waist. Triangular-shaped. Or maybe not. It's difficult to tell what a suit is disguising; it could be hiding a multitude of sins. But I hoped I was right.

Heat rose up my neck as he stared intently at me, his hand pushing his hair to one side. I offered a watery smile, before turning my head a full 360 degrees, looking for the voice.

"Is that a yes or no?" it said again, a little closer now. Mr. Peroni had maneuvered himself so that he was now my next-door neighbor but one. *What an odd expression that is*, I thought, oblivious to the fact that he was now standing right beside me. *Can you also have a next-door neighbor but two, and three?* I wondered.

"How many have you had?" He laughed as I continued to look at him blankly, though not without acknowledging that he was taller when he was close up.

"I'm sorry, I thought I heard someone call my name," I replied.

"I'm Adam," he offered.

"Oh. Emily," I said, thrusting out my hand, which had instantly become clammy. "I'm Emily."

"I know, it's written in rather large letters across your chest."

I looked down and felt myself flush. "Aha, so much for playing hard to get, eh?"

He tilted his head to one side, a naughty twinkle in his eye. "Who said we were playing?"

I had no idea whether we were or weren't. Flirting had never been my strong suit. I wouldn't know where to start, so if it was a game he was after, he was playing on his own.

"So, what's the deal with the name badge?" Mr. Peroni, aka Adam, asked, as coquettishly as a man can.

"I'm a member of an elite conference," I said, far more boldly than I felt.

"Is that so?" He smiled.

I nodded. "I'll have you know I'm the cream of the crop in my industry. One of the highest-ranking performers in the field."

"Wow." He smirked. "So, you're part of the Toilet Roll Sellers seminar? I saw the board for it when I walked in."

I suppressed a smile. "Actually, it's a secret meeting of MI5 agents," I whispered, looking around conspiratorially.

"And that's why they wrote your name all over your chest, is it? To make sure nobody finds out who you are."

I tried to keep a straight face, but the corners of my mouth were curling upward. "This is my undercover name," I said, tapping the cheap plastic. "My conference pseudonym."

"I see, Agent Emily," he said, rolling up his sleeve and talking into his watch. "So, is the gentleman at three o'clock also an agent?" He waited for me to catch up, but I didn't even know which way to look. I was twisting myself in every direction, haplessly trying to find three o'clock on my internal compass. He laughed as he caught hold of my shoulders and turned me to face Ivor, who was gesticulating wildly to a male colleague, while looking longingly at a female dressed in tight leather trousers behind him. She was happily unaware that his eyes were drinking her in. I shuddered involuntarily.

"Negative," I replied, one hand to my ear. "He is neither an agent nor a gentleman."

Adam laughed, as I warmed to the theme. "Can we class him as the enemy?"

"Affirmative. Take him down if you wish."

He squinted, in an effort to read the perpetrator's name badge. "Ivor?" he questioned.

I nodded.

"Ivor Biggun?" He looked at me, waiting for a reaction. It took me a while, a long while, in fact, to get it, but until I did, he just stood there, staring at me.

TWO

I wasn't looking for a boyfriend. I hadn't even known I'd wanted one until Adam showed up. Pippa, my flatmate, and I were blissfully content going to work, coming home, having our tea on trays, then gorging ourselves on chocolate while watching back-to-back episodes of *Prison Break*. It was heaven on earth for those few short hours, but the next morning I'd get on the scales and damn my nine pounds of winter weight gain. It was the same every year—and not helped by the fact that I never went to the gym that I paid seventy-two pounds a month for. I could no longer fit into the size-twelve jeans I'd worn the year before, but instead of buying myself a size fourteen, I'd scoured the shops to find a more generous size-twelve pair that I could pour myself into. I'd spent the entire summer "in denial," and was *still* kidding myself that the promised Indian summer would be sure to see my motivation return.

I would go out every once in a while, particularly around payday, but nights out weren't what they used to be. Maybe it was because I was getting older, or everyone else was getting younger, but I saw little benefit in standing in a crowded pub and having to elbow my way to the bar every time I wanted a drink. Pippa'd dragged me kicking and screaming to a few gigs, though not, unfortunately, at the O2 Arena. She favored underground caverns, where bands, most of whom she seemed to have slept with, thrashed about the stage and encouraged their audience to do the same. I was the one standing alone at the back, with hidden earphones blasting out *Musical Theater's Greatest Hits*.

Thank God for Seb, my best friend and a male version of me. I'd have married him years ago if I thought there was a single hair on his body that I could have turned straight, but, alas, I had to make do with evenings locked in a soundproof karaoke booth, each of us competing for the best lines in *Les Misérables*. We met during what he referred to as my "hairdressing period." Discontented with secretarial work, I'd booked myself on a night course for hair and beauty. Obviously, I had visions of becoming a female Vidal Sassoon, with a trendy salon in the middle of Mayfair and celebrity clients having to book months in advance. Instead, I spent three months sweeping up other people's hair and developing eczema on my hands from the caustic shampoo. I used to have these half-baked ideas and rush off to start making them happen, but I was forever deluded by grandeur. Like the time I enrolled on a homemaking course at my local college. It was never my intention to learn how to make a pretty cushion or spend hours rubbing five layers of eggshell off an old chest of drawers. No, I was going to bypass all the graft and groundwork that learning a new skill entailed. I was heading straight for New York, where I would be immediately commissioned to design a vast loft space for Chandler from *Friends*. Needless to say, the cushion never got finished and all the wallpaper samples and fabric swatches I'd acquired never saw the light of day again.

Seb had seen me through at least four career changes, and had been nothing short of overwhelmingly enthusiastic with each and every one, assuring me that I was "made for it." Yet, as each phase came and went and I'd be lamenting on the sofa at how useless I was, he'd convince me that I was never really cut out for it in the first place. But now I'd finally found my calling. It came a little later in life than I'd planned, but selling people was my thing. I knew what I was doing, and I was good at it.

"So, he's an IT analytical analyst?" Seb reiterated suspiciously, as we sat in Soho Square, sharing a sandwich and a salad bowl from M&S the following day. "Whatever that may mean."

I nodded enthusiastically, but inside I was asking myself the same question. I placed real people in real jobs: retail assistants in shops, secretaries in offices, dental assistants in medical offices. The IT sector was a whole new ball game, a monster of an industry, and one that we at Faulkner's left to the experts.

"Well, he sounds a right laugh-a-minute," Seb said, desperately trying to keep a straight face. "What did he do? Enthrall you with his megabytes?"

I laughed. "He doesn't look like you'd expect."

"So he doesn't wear glasses and have a center parting?"

I shook my head, smiling.

"And his name isn't Eugene?"

"No," I mumbled, through a mouthful of bread and roast beef. "He's tall and dark, with really good teeth."

"Oh, your mum will be pleased."

I swiped his shoulder with my hand. "And he's got a really sexy voice. All deep and mysterious. Like Matthew McConaughey, but without the Texan bit."

Seb raised his eyebrows quizzically. "Which would make him nothing like McConaughey."

I persisted. "You know what I mean. And big hands . . . really big hands, and nicely manicured nails."

"What the hell were you doing looking at his hands?" asked Seb, spluttering out his lemonade. "You were only with him for fifteen minutes, and you've already managed to check his cuticles out?"

I shrugged my shoulders petulantly. "I'm just saying that he obviously takes care of himself, and I like that in a man. It's important."

Seb tutted. "This all sounds very well, but on a scale of one to ten, how likely is it that you're going to see him again?"

"Honestly? A one or two. Firstly, he looked like the type to have a girlfriend, and secondly, I think he had his beer goggles on."

"Was he drunk or just merry?"

"Hard to tell. It was someone's leaving do, and I think he said something about coming from a pub in the City, so they'd obviously been going for a while. Adam looked okay, a bit disheveled, maybe, but then I don't know what he normally looks like. One or two of his mates were definitely well on their way, though—they could barely stand up."

"Oh, I bet the Grosvenor loved having *them* there," Seb said, laughing.

"I think they were asked to leave at the same time as I came away," I said, grimacing. "The well-heeled guests were starting to arrive, and the bar looked more like something on the Magaluf Strip than Park Lane."

"It's not looking good, kid," said Seb.

I wrinkled my nose. "No. I think the likelihood of hearing from him again is pretty slim."

"Did you give him the look?" he asked.

"What look?"

"You know the one. Your take-me-to-bed-or-lose-me-forever face?" He fluttered his eyelashes and licked his lips in the most unsexy way, like a dog after a chocolate-drop treat. He'd once been told by a potential suitor of mine that I had "bedroom eyes" and "engorged lips," and I'd not heard the last of it. "Well, did you?"

"Oh, shut up!"

"What were you wearing?" he asked.

I screwed my face up. "My black pencil skirt with a white blouse. Why?"

"He'll call you." He smiled. "If you'd been wearing that tent of a dress that you bought in the Whistles sale then I'd say you've got no chance, but in the pencil skirt? Moderate to high."

I laughed and threw a limp lettuce leaf at him. Every woman should have a Seb. He gave brutally honest advice, which on some days could send me off-kilter and have me reassessing my whole life, but today I was able to take it, happy to have him evaluate the situation because he was always darn well right.

"So, how are you going to play it when he calls?" he asked, retrieving the stray leaf from his beard and tossing it onto the grass.

"*If* he calls," I stressed, "I'll play it like I always do. Coy and demure."

Seb laughed and fell onto his back, tickling his ribs for added effect. "You are to coy and demure what I am to machismo."

I was tempted to empty the rest of the salad bowl onto his head as he lay writhing on the ground, but I knew it was likely to end up in a full-on food fight. I had a packed schedule that afternoon, and wanted to spare my silk shirt the onslaught of a balsamic-dressing attack. So, I gave him a playful nudge with the tip of my patent court shoe instead.

"Call yourself a friend?" I said haughtily, as I stood up to leave.

"Call me when he calls," Seb shouted out after me. He was still cackling as I walked away.

"I'll call you *if* he calls," I shouted back, as I reached the gates to the square.

I was in the middle of an appointment later that afternoon when my mobile rang. My client, a Chinese businessman who, with the help of a translator, was looking for staff for his expanding company, signaled to me to take it. I smiled politely and shook my head, but the "No Caller ID" displayed across the screen had piqued my interest. When it rang three more times, he looked at me imploringly, almost begging me to answer it.

"Excuse me," I said, before backing out of the room. It had better be important.

"Emily Havistock," I stated, as I swiped my iPhone.

"Havistock?" a voice repeated.

"Yes, can I help you?"

"No wonder they didn't put your surname on your badge." He laughed.

A redness crept up my neck, its fingers flickering at my cheeks. "I'm afraid I'm in a meeting at the moment. May I call you back?"

"I don't remember you sounding this posh either. Or is this your phone voice?"

I remained silent, but smiled.

"Okay, call me back," he said. "It's Adam, by the way. Adam Banks."

How many men does he think I give my number to?

"I'll text you," he said. "Just in case my number doesn't come up."

"Thank you, I'll revert to you shortly," I said, terminating the call, but not before I heard him chuckle.

I couldn't concentrate for the rest of the appointment, and found myself trying to wrap it up prematurely. But then, I didn't want to appear over-keen by calling him back too quickly, so when the translator said my client would like to show me around the new office space a few floors above, I gratefully accepted.

Over dinner, a week later, I had to explain to Adam why it had taken me three hours to call him back.

"You honestly expect me to believe that?" he asked incredulously.

"I swear to you. I'm not one for holding out just to appear cool. Making you sweat for an hour, perhaps. But three? That's just rude." I laughed.

His eyes wrinkled up as he tried to suppress a smile. "And you were seriously stuck in a lift for all that time?"

"Yes, for three *really* long hours, with a man who hardly spoke English, and two super-smart phones, neither of which were smart enough to be able to ring for help, it seems."

He choked on his sauvignon blanc and spluttered, "That's Chinese technology for you."

By the time I introduced Adam to Seb, a month later, we'd seen each other eighteen times.

"Are you serious?" Seb had moaned, when I'd told him for the third consecutive night that I couldn't see him. "When do you think you might be able to fit me in?"

"Ah, don't go getting all jealous," I'd teased. "Maybe tomorrow night?"

"If he doesn't ask to see you again then, I suppose?"

"I promise, tomorrow night is yours and yours alone." Though, even as I was saying it, I felt a tad resentful.

"Okay, what do you want to do?" he asked sulkily. "That film's out— of the book that we both loved."

"*The Fault in Our Stars*?" I said, without thinking. "Adam and I are going to see that tonight."

"Oh." I could feel his disappointment, and I instantly wanted to slap myself.

"But that's okay," I said cheerily. "I'll go again tomorrow night. The book was amazing, so the film will be too, right? We've *got* to see it together."

"If you're sure . . ." Seb said, his voice lifting. "Try not to enjoy it too much with your boyfriend."

If only I could. I was too conscious of Adam fidgeting in his seat, look-ing at his phone. "Well, that was a happy little tale," he said, as we came out of the cinema a couple of hours later.

"It's all right for you," I said, sniffing and surreptitiously wiping my nose on a tissue. "I've got to go through it all again tomorrow."

He stopped in the street and turned to look at me. "Why?" he asked.

"Because I've promised Seb I'll go and see it with him."

Adam raised his eyebrows questioningly.

"We both loved the book and always vowed that when they made the film, we'd see it together."

"But you've seen it now," he said. "Job done."

"I know, but it's something we both wanted to do."

"I need to meet this Seb who's taking you away from me," he said, pulling me toward him and breathing in my hair.

"If he was straight, you'd have a problem on your hands," I said, laughing. "But you've got nothing to worry about."

"All the same. Let's get together one night next week so that we can all discuss the merits and flaws of the silly film we've just seen."

I playfully punched him on the arm, and he kissed me on the head. It felt like we'd been together forever, yet the excitement of just being around him fizzed through me, setting every nerve alight. I didn't ever want that feeling to go away.

It was way too early to tell, but there was a growing part of me, the part that no one saw, that hoped this *was* something. I wasn't brave enough, or stupid enough, perhaps, to be singing from the rooftops that Adam was "the one," but I liked how it felt. It felt different, and I had all my fingers and toes crossed that my hunch was right.

We were comfortable with each other, not to the point where I'd leave the bathroom door open, but I wasn't obsessing about whether my nail color matched my lip shade either, and not many guys had been around long enough to see them clashing.

"Are you sure it's not too early for the Seb-o-meter?" Seb asked, wiping his eyes as we walked out of the same cinema twenty-four hours later. "I mean, it's not even been a month yet, has it?"

"Well, thanks for your vote of confidence," I said. I was sniveling again too, but, as I was with Seb, it didn't matter. I put my arm through his, uniting us in our sadness at how the film had ended.

"I don't mean to sound negative, but it's all a bit full-on to last, don't you think? You're seeing him almost every night. Are you sure it won't just fizzle out as quickly as it started? Don't forget, I know what you're like."

I smiled, despite feeling a little hurt at the insinuation that what Adam and I had could be just a fling. "I've never felt like this, Seb. I need you to meet him because I think this might be going somewhere. And it's important to me that you like him."

"But you know you're going to get a very honest appraisal," he went on. "Are you ready for that?"

"I think you're going to like him," I said. "And if you don't, just pretend you do."

He laughed. "Is there any topic that's off-limits? Like the time you asked me to marry you, or when you threw your knickers at Justin Timberlake?"

I laughed. "No, it's all good. You can say whatever you want. There's nothing I wouldn't want him to know."

"Hang on," said Seb, as he bent forward and made a retching sound. "There. That's better. Where were we?"

"D'you know that you're a right royal pain in the arse when you want to be?" I laughed.

"You wouldn't want me any other way."

"Seriously, he's pretty laid-back, so I don't think you'll be able to faze him that easily."

That was the only thing with Adam: If he was any more laid-back he'd be horizontal. In his world, everything was calm and under control, like a sea without waves. He didn't get exasperated when we were stuck behind a painfully slow driver. He didn't call southeastern trains every name under the sun when leaves on the track caused delays, and he didn't blame social media for everything that was wrong with the world. "If you don't like what it represents, why do you go on it?" he'd asked, when I moaned about old school friends posting every burp, fart, and word their child offered.

None of the trivial stuff that had me spitting tacks almost every minute of my day seemed to touch him. Maybe he was sitting back, carefully navigating his way around my own waves and currents before revealing his own, but I wanted him to give me more. I needed to know that blood coursed through his veins and that he'd bleed if he cut himself.

I'd tried to provoke a reaction from him several times, even if just to check that he had a pulse, but I wasn't going to get a rise out of him. He seemed happy just ambling along, with no real need or desire to offer anything more. Maybe I was being unfair, maybe that was just the way he was, but every now and again I liked to be challenged, even if it was only a debate over an article in the *Daily Mail*. It wouldn't matter what it was, just anything that would give me an insight into his world. But no matter how hard I tried, we always ended up talking about me, even when I was the one asking the questions. There was no denying that, at times, it was a refreshing change, as the last guy I'd gone out with had prattled on about his video-game obsession all night. But Adam's constant deflection left me wondering: What did I *really* know about him?

That was why I needed Seb. He was the type of person who could get right in there, burrow his way through the complex layers of people's characters and into their souls, which they were often baring within minutes of meeting him. He'd once asked my mother if my dad was the only man she'd ever been with. I'd immediately put my hands over my ears and la-la-la-ed, but she confessed to having had a wonderful affair with an American she met, just before her and Dad got together. "Well, it wasn't the type of affair that you youngsters talk about nowadays," she said. "We didn't have clandestine meetings and illicit sex, and neither of us were married, so it wasn't an affair in the sense that *you* know. It was just a beautiful meeting of two people who were utterly in tune with each other."

My mouth had dropped open. Aside from the shock that my mother had obviously had sex more than twice, from which she'd conceived me and my brother, it had been with someone *other* than my father? As a daughter, you so rarely get to discover these golden gems of times gone by, and before we know it, it's too late to ask. But when you're with someone like Seb, every little nugget is teased out, without you even realizing.

The following weekend, Adam, Seb, and I arranged to meet in a bar in Covent Garden. I didn't like to suggest dinner, just in case it felt a little forced and awkward, but I was hoping that was how the evening would end up organically. We'd not even finished our first drink before Seb asked Adam where he grew up.

"Just outside Reading," he replied. "We moved down to Sevenoaks when I was nine. What about you?"

There it was again.

But Seb wasn't going to be thwarted. "I was born in Lewisham hospital, and have stayed there ever since. Not in the hospital, obviously, but literally just two roads down, off the High Street. I went to Sevenoaks a couple of years ago; a guy I was seeing had a design consultancy down there. Very pretty. What made you move there from Reading?"

Adam shifted uncomfortably. "Erm, my dad died. Mum had friends in Sevenoaks and needed a bit of help with me and my younger brother. There was nothing to stay in Reading for. Dad had worked for Microsoft for years, but with him gone . . ." He trailed off.

"Yeah, I lost my dad too," offered Seb. "Crap, eh?"

Adam gave a sad nod.

"So, is your mum still on her own, or did she meet someone else?" asked Seb, before guiltily adding, "Sorry, I assume your mum's still around?"

Adam nodded. "Yes, thank God. She's still in Sevenoaks and still on her own."

"It's difficult when they're on their own, isn't it?" asked Seb. "You feel a lot more responsible for them, even when you're the child and they're supposed to be the grown-up."

Adam raised his eyebrows and nodded in agreement. I couldn't add to this conversation as thankfully both my parents were still alive, so I offered to get a round in instead.

"No, I'll get them," said Adam, no doubt relieved to extract himself from Seb's searching questions. "Same again?"

Seb and I nodded.

"So . . . ?" I asked, as soon as Adam's back was turned.

"Very nice," Seb said. "Very nice."

"But?" I sensed one coming.

"I'm not sure," he said, as my heart sank. "There's something, but I can't quite put my finger on it."

That night, after we'd made love and were lying side by side, tracing our fingers over each other's torsos, I raised the subject of his parents again.

"Do you think your mother will like me?" I asked.

He rolled over and pushed himself up onto one elbow. The light was off, but the curtains were open and the moon was bright. I could see his silhouette close to me, feel his breath on my face. "Of course she would. She'd think you're perfect."

I couldn't help but notice the turn of phrase: "she'd" instead of "she'll." There's a big difference between the two—one hypothetical, the other intentional. The sentence spoke volumes.

"So, you're not planning on introducing us anytime soon, then?" I asked, as lightly as I could.

"We've only been together for a month." He sighed, sensing the weight of the question. "Let's just take our time, see how it goes."

"So, I'm good enough to sleep with, but not to meet your mother?"

"You're good enough for both." He laughed. "Let's just take it slowly. No pressure. No promises."

I fought the tightness at the back of my throat and turned away from him. *No pressure. No promises?* What was this? And why did it matter so much? I could count on two hands how many lovers I'd had. Every one of them had meant something, apart from a shockingly uncharacteristic one-night stand I'd had at a friend's twenty-first birthday.

But despite having been in love and lust before, I couldn't ever remember feeling this safe. And that was how Adam made me feel. He made me feel all of the above. Every little box had a tick in it and, for the first time in my adult life, I felt whole, as if all the jigsaw pieces had been slotted into place.

"Okay," I said, annoyed at my own neediness. I would have gladly shown him off to my mother's half aunt's second cousin twice removed. Clearly, he didn't feel the same, and, despite myself, it hurt.

THREE

A horn blared.

Pippa, who was hanging out the window sneaking a cigarette, shouted, "Your boyfriend's here, in his posh car."

"Ssh," I retorted. "He'll hear you."

"He's three floors down. And half the bloody street can hear *him*, so I wouldn't worry about it."

I squeezed through the same window and gave him a wave. He tooted back, and Bill, our next-door neighbor, looked up from washing his car. "It's all right, Bill," Pippa shouted down. "It's Emily's fancy man."

Bill shrugged and got back to the task in hand. He was the best type of neighbor you could have: keeping a lookout when he needed to, and turning a blind eye when he didn't.

Pippa and I weren't the typical demographic for the area; young married couples, with 2.5 children, were the norm. They claimed to love Lee, this diverse enclave between Lewisham and Blackheath, but we and they knew they were just biding their time until they were able to climb that very big step up to the latter. Blackheath was where everyone wanted to be, with its quirky village feel and vast open spaces. They say that the plague victims of the seventeenth century were buried up on Blackheath, hence the name, but it didn't bother people enough to stop them from holding impromptu barbecues on a summer's evening. Many a time, Pippa and I had joined the masses pretending to live there, by lighting up a camping stove under a disposable foil tray that we'd hastily bought at the petrol station. We always ended up arriving too late to get the best spots by the pubs, and by the time we'd trusted the British weather, it was gone four P.M. and the supermarket BBQ section had been stripped bare.

"Ooh, you look nice," remarked Pippa.

I smoothed down the front of my bodycon dress, even though there was nothing to smooth down. "You think?"

I'd spent the best part of an hour choosing what to wear, agonizing between the casualness of a pretty blouse and white jeans, and the more formal look of a structured dress. I didn't want to look like I'd tried too hard, but not making enough effort was probably worse, so the navy dress won out. The crêpe cinched in at my waist, out again over my hips, and fell just below the knee. There was just the tiniest amount of cleavage showing, and the fabric shaped my breasts perfectly. As my mother would say, "That dress hangs in all the right places."

"Nervous?" asked Pippa.

"I'm all right, actually," I lied. She didn't need to know that a further hour had been spent on blow-drying my hair, putting it up, then down, then up again. It was longer than it had been in quite a while, falling just below my shoulders, and I'd had a few highlights pulled through my natural auburn color to give it a lift. I'd settled on pinning it up, and had coaxed a couple of loose curls to fall on either side of my face to soften the look. The French manicure I'd had done a couple of days before was holding up well, and I'd kept my makeup light and natural. Effortlessly chic was the image I was going for—I was, after all, only meeting my boyfriend's mother—but in reality I'd done less preparation for a good friend's wedding.

"Good luck," she called out as I reached the front door. "She's going to love you."

I wished that I shared her confidence.

I caught sight of Adam watching me as I walked down the path with a bouquet in my hand, and emphasized my strut. "Whoa, you look gorgeous," he said, as I got in and leaned over to give him a kiss. It went on a little longer than we'd expected and I lambasted him for ruining my lipstick.

"Yeah, you might need to reapply that," he said, smiling as he wiped his lips. "You got a spare pair of tights as well?" His hand traveled up between my legs. "Just in case I rip these."

I looked up at Bill, who was buffing his car's hood, and playfully swiped Adam's hand away. "Will you stop it? The poor man's already had one heart attack. I don't want to give him another."

"It's probably the most action he's seen in years." He laughed.

I tutted and carefully laid the flowers on the backseat. "Trying to impress someone, are we?" he asked, smiling.

"Oh, ha-bloody-ha," I said.

"You feel okay about this?" He reached over and took my hand in his.

"A little bit sick," I replied honestly. "I've only ever met one mum before."

He laughed. "That couldn't have gone too well, then, if you're here with me."

I gave him a playful dig. "It's a big deal. If she doesn't like me, I'm doomed. You probably won't even give me a lift back."

"She'll love you," he said, going to ruffle my hair.

I caught his hand in midair. "Don't even think about it. Do you have any idea how long this updo has taken?"

"Bloody hell, you don't even make this much effort when you're going out with *me*. Maybe I should introduce you to my mum more often." He laughed.

"I don't need to impress you anymore," I said. "I've got you wrapped around my little finger, right where I want you. It's your mum I need to get under my spell now. If I can get her on my side, I can rule the world." I let out a sinister cackle.

"I've told her you're normal. You'd better start acting like it."

"You've told her I'm normal?" I shrieked in mock protest. "Well, that doesn't make me sound very exciting, does it? Couldn't you have sexed it up a bit?" I watched his face break into a grin. "What else have you said about me?"

He thought for a moment. "That you're funny, clever, and can make a mean English breakfast."

"Adam!" I moaned. "Is that it? Is that all I am to you? A purveyor of sausages?"